Dedication

This book is dedicated to three of my greatest teachers,

Jonathon Smith, who taught me about genuine friendship
Hal Kelly, who taught me about the importance of love
"John" Islwyn Jenkins, who taught me to be myself

Acknowledgements

I wish to express my grateful thanks to my many clients who have provided me with the opportunities to hone my skills, which are the foundations of this book. I would especially like to thank Ed MacAlister Smith and Andrea Young for providing me with the opportunity to test drive this work.

My sincere thanks go to Bob Maher for his continued encouragement and to Trevor Walker for seeing the potential of our collaboration.

I would like to thank my Father, John Edwards for giving me the determination to succeed, and my Mother, June Edwards for providing me with a happy and secure childhood. These have been and continue to be the foundations of my life. I love you both.

I would particularly like to acknowledge my husband Robert Moeller. We have traversed many of life's storms together, and having you by my side has allowed me to grow and flourish. I love you all-ways.

I am greatly indebted to you all, thank you for being a part of my life.

The Barefoot Executive
Leadership Skills for the 21ˢᵗ Century

Linda Edwards

Eloquent Books

New York, New York

Eloquent Books
New York, New York

Eloquent Books
An imprint of AEG Publishing Group
845 Third Avenue, 6th Floor - 6016
New York, NY 10022
www.EloquentBooks.com

ISBN: 978-1-60693-819-5
SKU: 1-60693-819-3

Printed in the United States of America

Book design by Wendy Arakawa

Table of Contents

Introduction

This book is based on my experience of working within and alongside numerous organizations. My direct experience of being a leader combined with being a coach to many chief executives and directors has highlighted the multitude of struggles people face within these roles. The fundamental issue is that people over complicate situations, and find themselves tied into the 'tick tock' of the daily grind. By helping people to lift themselves out of tick-tock, I've been able to help them to see the bigger picture, and the purpose of their actions and re-actions.

In modern business today, people spend so much time re-acting to things outside of themselves, they forget their overall purpose. Tick tock takes over, causing people to relinquish control, and to spend their time focusing on the symptoms of issues rather than cutting through to the real root cause. It's the same as when a doctor treats a physical dis-ease, often treating the symptoms without always knowing the cause. It's the same with organizational dis-ease, people spend so much time focusing on the symptoms, the tick tock, that they fail to see the bigger picture, and the "thing" that caused the problem in the first place. By focusing on tick tock we create even more tick tock until we feel like we're drowning in it.

This book is a metaphor, which brings together the experiences of many senior executives enabling you to go on a

◆

journey of discovery from the land of tick-tock into the land of purpose and cause. Maxine is a newly appointed chief executive who faces the challenges of turning around an ailing organization. The employees are unhappy and do the minimum amount of work they can get away with. Her challenge is to change this "dinosaur" into a highly productive, vibrant organization, one where people enjoy coming to work and where they are appreciated for their individual and collective talents.

We travel with Maxine through her early encounters with her new staff, and their initial reluctance to move out of tick and tock to face the challenges involved in doing this. It's a story many leaders and managers will be able to relate to, showing the importance of retaining a true sense of purpose and mission as an organizational leader.

Finally, Maxine combines her own innate understanding of psychology with her management training and the assistance of her coach, to create a supportive, caring organization that delivers the seemingly impossible, out performing its competitors time and time again.

Barefoot is about the ability to combine the essence of who we are (our true self) with our intellectual self. This enables our conscious mind (the director) to build a true partnership with our unconscious mind (the home of our intuition). By allowing this connection to take place, and be a part of our lives, leadership and management become a part of who we are rather than what we do.

My intention in writing this book is to motivate you to nurture your own leadership and management style, combining heart and mind to create approaches to leadership and management that enable you to be truly 'barefoot' and to succeed.

I wish you every success,

Linda Edwards

Marston, Wiltshire

Part 1 -The Boardroom

1

In The Beginning

Maxine drove into the parking lot of Extreme Ventures Ltd., parked her car, and switched off the engine. She sighed, and said quietly to herself, "Here you are on day one of being the new Chief Executive. So, let's go turn this place around." She took a deep breath to calm herself, checked her long hair in the mirror, and climbed out of the car.

Intuitively, Maxine knew that she was about to start a big adventure as the new chief executive of Extreme Ventures Ltd. The company had a reputation for being very traditional, which she thought was interesting, given its name. The problem had been that the last Chief Executive had diligently stuck to old 20th century approaches to business with the result that the staff were disenchanted, productivity was at an all-time low, and employees were leaving in droves. Maxine had applied for the job as she relished a new challenge; she had spent the last twelve years as a management consultant. During this time she had learned a great deal about organizations, and how they functioned. Prior to this, she had been a director and chief executive in a large corporation. Since then, she had invested substantially in her own development. She had also just completed a transforming personal development program and was very eager to implement all her new knowledge in an environment where change was essential for survival. Now she very much wanted to implement massive change whilst being the hands steering the entire change process at Extreme Ventures Ltd.

Maxine's mind was full of exciting thoughts as she opened the front door to enter Extreme Ventures Ltd. She smiled at the receptionist, said "Good morning," and walked up the single flight of stairs to her office. Candice, her "new" secretary was there to greet her, with a warm if somewhat hesitant smile. As she stood up, Maxine saw a smartly-dressed young woman of around twenty-five with blonde hair tied back in a ponytail. She said, "Good morning," and asked if Maxine would like some coffee. Maxine nodded and smiled appreciatively. While Candice went to make the coffee, Maxine walked through the door into her office, and looked around. The energy in the large modern room was heavy, and the whole room felt uncomfortable. It felt old and distinctly cold.

Maxine shuddered slightly as she sat at the desk. The room was arranged like a fortress. She found herself seated in a huge black leather chair, peering out from behind the biggest desk she had ever seen. There was at least six feet between her and whoever would sit on the considerably smaller chair opposite.

Wow, she thought, what a way to operate. She twirled playfully in the chair, stopping opposite a large conference table that was attached to the left side of this vast desk. The diameter of this was at least eight feet across. The floor-to-ceiling bookshelves opposite were dark and domineering. Maxine went over to examine them and found that they were full of ancient, thick, hard-backed books full of models of twentieth century management models. There was even one called *The Management Skills of Attila the Hun.*

As Maxine was contemplating the culture of her new organization and beginning to wonder what lay ahead of her there was a knock on her office door. When she called, "Come in," Candice entered with a bone china cup and saucer accompanied by a bone china plate of cookies. Maxine looked at the young woman's expectant face and wide open blue eyes, and thought, what kind of a world have I come into here?

"Thank you, Candice," she said. "Could you please bring my schedule so that we can talk about my induction program, and anything important I must do this week?"

Candice rapidly reappeared with a diary and notepad, looking very nervous she sat in the smaller chair opposite Maxine and waited.

Maxine smiled at her and said, "You and I will need to work closely together so I'd like us to agree the best way to do this." Candice looked at Maxine with wide eyes, and an expression that appeared to be a combination of confusion and fear, but said nothing.

Remembering the voice of her coach, and the importance of building rapport, Maxine said, "I think you'll   find, that I probably have a different management style from my predecessor. So I think it'd be a good idea for us to agree on the best way to work together, what do you think?"

Candice gulped and said, "Yes." Candice's surprised face caused Maxine to realize that she was going to have to pace this quite carefully.

Sipping her coffee Maxine said, "Shall I tell you how I like to work? Would that be helpful?"

"Yes, please," came the quiet reply.

"OK, well as chief executive, I view my role as someone who enables others to do their jobs effectively. I'm also responsible for providing leadership, which involves ensuring that the framework is in place in order to do this. I also want to ensure that *everyone* who works here is aware of the vision and overall direction of the company along with their own contribution to this. I feel that it's fundamental to the success of the organization that people are able to speak freely and actively participate in the development, future and vision of the organization as a whole."

"What vision?" blurted Candice suddenly.

"I was shown the organizational vision at my interview," said Maxine, somewhat perplexed, "Are you telling me that you don't know what it is?"

"No, I mean yes," said Candice. "I didn't know we had one. Mr. Prentice never said anything about a vision." No wonder the company is floundering, thought Maxine, it seems as if I've let myself in for more of a challenge than I thought. She took another sip of her coffee as she gathered her thoughts. Steady on, she reminded herself. I had better reserve judgement for a while until I've met the top team.

She looked up to see the younger woman studying her

carefully "Candice," she said "I want to meet as many people as possible as quickly as possible to enable me to develop an understanding of the overall work of Extreme Ventures. This will then enable us to build a new vision of the future for the organization, a vision that everyone understands, and is a part of. "So will you please arrange for me to meet each of the directors individually this week for at least an hour. I'd initially like to meet them in their offices, and for them to show me around their departments."

"You mean you don't want them to come here to your office?" questioned Candice. "Mr. Prentice never went to other people's offices, except the chairman's of course."

"Yes, I want to meet them in their offices so I can see how everything fits together, then we can meet in my office later," replied Maxine. She then logged a private thought; it looks as if we have an organization based on hierarchy rather than competence here.

"Candice please give me a few moments, and then I'd like you to give me a tour of the organization, so that I can meet as many people as possible.

◆

I'll then start my more in-depth introductions this afternoon. I also want you to arrange a full staff meeting for nine o'clock tomorrow so that I can introduce myself and share my thoughts with everyone about the future."

In her experience, Maxine had come across many organizations that were ailing, a number of whom hid their problems behind a system of hierarchy. "You do as I say" was the motto. In these organizations there was little engagement with the workforce, and hence everyone operated as an individual instead of valued members of a team or group of teams. The result was a typical cycle of poor performance, more dictatorial instructions, a reduction in morale, and another performance drop. It looks as if I'll have some fun here turning this one around thought Maxine with a rye smile, and it's only nine thirty in the morning.

Maxine heard Candice's voice, bringing her out of her reverie "Shall I go and set up the appointments for you?"

"Yes please Candice." By now Maxine knew she needed to do something about the style of her office sooner rather than later. It was clear that when people came into the office they would be anchored to the feelings that they used to feel with Mr Prentice. Maxine realized that she needed to change these factors quickly to remove the previous emotional anchors, and to enable people to operate in a new way.

She was quickly getting the impression that things needed to change at a deeply fundamental level. Aware that hasty decisions could create more mayhem, she decided to wait until she had met the top team before making any fundamental decisions. However, her first thirty minutes were indicating that something radical would need to be done, and done soon. She knew that she needed to garner as much information as possible to enable her to present an outline proposal to the board at her first board meeting in three weeks time.

LEARNING POINTS

➤   Fundamental to effective communication is the need to build rapport and pace people

➤   Meet people on their own territory rather than hiding behind your own desk in your own territory. This enables you to see people in their own environment, and to develop an appreciation of how they operate.

➤   In a new role meet as many people as possible as quickly as possible.

➤   Remove as many "anchors" as possible left by any predecessor. Move or replace furniture to create your own relationships without any anchors related to past experiences.

2

Meeting the Players

Maxine sat back in her large black leather chair and chuckled gently to herself, well girl, you said you wanted a challenge it looks as if you have certainly got one here. Her smile broadened as she remembered the voice of Colin, her coach saying,

"Remember for the first week or so, simply ask questions and listen. The downfall of many a new chief executive has been impulsive actions based on flimsy information, and a lack of understanding of the organizational culture. Listen with your full attention, take copious notes if you need to and see the patterns emerging within the overall picture. Once you see the bigger picture clearly, you will see the changes that need

to be made and the levers to pull to initiate this change. Remember, if you feel yourself getting drawn into tick-tock, STOP, take a deep breath, release it slowly and stand back. From this dissociated and more distant perspective you will be able to make better informed decisions."

His wise words rang in Maxine's head as she prepared for her first "walk about". Tick–tock was a term Colin used to describe being drawn into unnecessary detail which pulls your attention away from the truly important issues. Maxine also knew that the informal discussions on her walk-abouts would reveal much to her about the organizational culture. She was excited and intrigued by what she might find. She was also looking forward to her coaching session with Colin next week when she would be able to share her insights and revelations.

Candice knocked at the door and came back into the room, "Miss Brown, are you ready to sound things out around the building?"

Maxine smiled warmly, and said "Candice please call me Maxine, Miss Brown sounds rather like I'm one of my old school teachers."

Candice blushed, and said coyly, "Ok, Maxine are you ready?" Maxine nodded, and the two women set off on their walk-about.

Maxine thought, this is really great. I'm already beginning to understand the best way to communicate with Candice effectively. I need to use auditory type words such as "sounds like", "resonate" and "tune in" so that she can hear (understand) what I have to say. Maxine knew that different people use different predicates (types of words) and the importance of using those predicates when communicating with them. She therefore made a mental note to listen carefully to people's predicates.

◆

Their first stop was the main operations department, which was headed up by James, the Director of Operations. The initial impact on Maxine was one of total chaos. James seemed to have papers piled up everywhere in his office, and the whole department seemed to be full of heaps of paper. There were papers on the floor, piled up on desks, and falling into paper cascades as the piles toppled over. Maxine asked a few questions and was introduced to the team leaders all of whom seemed to view her with a strange reserve. She felt as if she had landed from Mars. My goodness, she thought, how can they ever find anything in those mountains of paperwork?

As she left the department Maxine realized that she had not seen one person in the whole department smile, they seemed to be literally, physically weighed down by the mountains of paper.

Next, she went into the post room, and was horrified to see the mail boxes overflowing and bulging with yet more paper. Maxine took a deep breath and asked, "How does the postal system work?"

"We collect the post from the departments, frank it and bag it" came the rather vague reply. Maxine got the distinct impression that there did not appear to be any cohesion in the way the whole department had been set up. She also discovered that they had not been able to recruit to position of department manager for over a year. No wonder they appear to be completely rudderless and chaotic, she thought as John, the man who was

◆

working the 'steam driven' franking machine explained how he franked the day's mail.

Maxine's next visit was to the contracting department. The director Jill, a very neat and tidy middle-aged woman explained how contracts were set up and renewed. Again the whole department seemed to be drowning under the weight of paper. Maxine enquired about performance monitoring processes, and was met with blank stares. Is there anywhere in this organization that is functioning effectively, she wondered.

Moving on into the last department, finance and information management, Maxine was delighted to see an almost paper free zone. However, Richard, the director, a pale drawn intense man seemed reluctant to answer basic questions about processes and procedures. I wonder what he is afraid of? thought Maxine.

As she returned to her office with Candice she asked "What happens about customer services? I didn't see any evidence of anyone with that brief?"

"Oh, I do that when I get a moment," said Candice smiling widely.

What does she actually do in these moments thought Maxine? Her mind was racing, the main crux of this organization was about providing services to customers, and the chief executive's PA did it 'when she got a moment'.

Aaargh, thought Maxine. What have I really inherited

◆

here? I'm really going to have
to do some radical re-thinking.
But where do I start? One thing
is for sure, if I'm ever to secure
the success of this organization I
need to place the customer at it's
very heart.

Once again she heard Colin's voice in her head. "Stop,
look and listen. Once you have a clear picture then you start to
plan your actions, and *only then*. By jumping in with both feet
you will cause more problems than you solve. Your first task is to
set about winning the hearts and minds of your people, to harness
their energy and commitment.
You need to prove to them that
you're a leader worth following,
someone who will guide and steer
them to success, and personal
pride in their work. Start one step
at a time. Remember every great
journey starts with a single step."

Hearing Colin's grounding words enabled Maxine to
relax, breathe and reflect on all she had heard.

I wonder how I'm going to unpick all of this, and turn
this place around. I need to assess the top team quickly, and
agree an approach to improve performance. That is if anyone
knows what the current position is. I wonder what ideas they
have. I also need to take every opportunity to lift the energy of

this place if I'm to succeed in my mission. It seems a little like the statement at the beginning of Star Trek 'To go where no man has ever gone before.' Maxine giggled to herself, I can see I'm going to need a good sense of humor here.

It was a lovely sunny day so Maxine decided to take a walk down to the river at lunchtime to eat her sandwich, and reflect on her first morning. She sat on a bench in the sunshine, and watched the swans swimming along, while she enjoyed the warmth of the sun. She realized that she felt peaceful, and yet excited at the same time, her concerns about taking on this job were ebbing with every minute that passed. One thing was certain; she was beginning to think that Extreme Ventures was aptly named as extreme action was definitely called for.

JAMES, DIRECTOR OF OPERATIONS

That afternoon Maxine met with James the Director of Operations. He arrived in her office and sat on the far side of the huge desk with a note pad and pen poised as if to take short hand notes. Maxine walked around and pulled up a chair next to him, thinking to herself, I need to get a couple of arm chairs in here quickly because this desk provides such a barrier to communication.

"James, I suspect my style of leadership is different from my predecessor," she said. "The way that I see it, my job is to help

◆

you to do your job as effectively as possible. Therefore, I need you to explain to me everything that goes on in your department, and how you measure success. I also need to understand the organizational structure beneath you, what works well, and what areas if any, need improvement."

Maxine listened attentively as James described the work of his department, the people and processes. As she listened she focused on the words that James used, knowing that his speech patterns and words would give her great insights into the way she would need to manage and coach him. He seemed to lack any real focus, and she saw no demonstrable evidence of leadership skills. She soon realized that she needed to ask very specific questions to prevent the conversation being full of details that

meant nothing to her. The main function of the operations department was to transfer documentation from one client organization to another when needed, to log activity and to arrange for the appropriate fees to be paid for claims received.

"So what are the three major challenges that you face in the department?" asked Maxine steering the conversation to be more specific.

"It has been really hard recently as we seem to have lost at least 150 client records and claims in the last two months." He replied.

Maxine caught her breath and gulped. The loss of records

◆

would have a huge impact on the clients involved. She calmed herself, exhaled slowly, and said, "Ok, so what have you done to rectify this matter?"

"Oh, I felt the only thing we could do was to employ temporary staff to go through all of the files so that we can find the missing ones," came the reply.

Remembering the piles of paper in the department Maxine then asked, "So what steps have been taken to ensure these mistakes are not repeated?"

"Well, I haven't had time to do that," replied James. "All the complaints we've been receiving have taken up all of my time."

Once again, Maxine took a deep breath to center herself. She resisted the temptation to leap in and solve the problem herself, and so she said, "I want you to think about at least three different ways in which you can solve this problem and prevent it from re-occurring. Then I'd like you to come back to discuss this with me after the staff meeting tomorrow. The sooner we can agree a way to resolve this, and let our clients know what we're doing to rectify the situation the better. What are the clients saying at the moment?"

"I don't really know" replied James, "we don't actually know until someone complains, and then we can do something. We just have too much work to be able to do anything else. I feel that if I could have more staff it would be better."

◆

I need to know how he assesses his own performance, thought Maxine and then said, "Tell me James, how do you know when you have done a good job?"

"I'd hope you or somebody else would tell me," he replied.

"Ok," said Maxine logging this important information. "We really do need to get a feel for the volume of work that's required to resolve this matter. So, I need you to come back with three solutions tomorrow, and to bring as much performance information as you have. We can then agree the best course of action."

"Ok," said a rather bewildered-looking James. "But how will I know I'm identifying the right solutions?"

"Remember I've asked for three possible solutions," said Maxine. "We can then evaluate the impact of each of these together. Then we can inform our clients about what we're doing, and the reasons for doing it."

As James left the office Maxine wrote down her assessment. James was highly kinesthetic in his speech (he used a lot of feeling type words), he had been in the same type of job for over 20 years, and therefore would probably find change challenging. He appeared to lack any vision, and seemed very stuck. From what he had told her, his career had simply 'happened' by being 'nice' and being in the 'right place' at the 'right time'.

Ok Max, she said to herself. What does this mean in respect to how I need to manage James? He is kinesthetic, so I need to use 'feeling type' words like comfortable, tough, hard, soft, and he will literally need time to take in the information, and try it on for size. He will need regular feedback on his progress, and as he has done the same type of work for so long it will be important to tell him what will be the same or remain unchanged in any change process. Now, have I missed anything?

Yes, I also need to give him feedback as he needs external validation. Good, I think I have that one sorted out for now.

Maxine wrote in her notebook, *James – kinesthetic, sameness, needs external validation.*

As Maxine closed her book she thought, if this initial meeting is anything to go by, I can see that life is going to be really interesting here. I wonder if all of the departments are as chaotic as the operations teams?

With that thought she looked at her watch, and saw that she had thirty minutes before her next appointment. "Time to do something about this office," she said out loud to herself. She popped her head around the door, and said to Candice, "Please make sure I'm not disturbed for the next twenty minutes, I have work to do."

Whilst allowing her assessment of James to percolate into her mind, Maxine looked around her office. The energy felt so heavy and unwelcoming that she decided she needed to do something immediately to lighten it up. She would need to acquire some more welcoming furniture quickly that would enable people to relax and be themselves. At the moment it felt very much like being summoned into the headmistress' room. By changing the furniture and introducing a more welcoming atmosphere, Maxine knew that she would be removing the negative anchors left by her predecessor. In this way she could assist people in developing new feelings (anchors) associated with her and her tenure. In the meantime she needed to do something about the room to lift the oppressiveness. She had been trained in several energy cleansing techniques, and decided it was really important to use these now to free the room from the 'heaviness' of her predecessor. Maxine centered herself and took several long deep breaths before she carried out an

ancient Hawaiian process for cleansing and releasing energy. As she opened her eyes Maxine could feel that the oppression had been lifted from the room.

"Ah, that feels much better," she said with a gentle sigh. Looking at her watch she saw that it was almost three o'clock, and time to meet with Jill.

JILL, DIRECTOR OF CONTRACTS

Jill arrived on the stroke of three. As she came into Maxine's office she said, "What have you done in this room, it looks really different?"

"I'm just starting to make it my own. I decided it was a little too oppressive for my taste," she replied. She knew that the concept of energy cleansing was a bit "far out" for some people, so had decided that discretion was the better part of valor at this early stage.

Maxine walked around and joined Jill on the other side of the desk whilst asking her to describe the work of her department. Jill started to talk in a lot of detail about the actual processes in her department. As she did this Maxine was paying attention not only to what she was saying but also the words and speech patterns that would give her Jill's operating strategies.

As Jill came to a natural pause, Maxine asked her "So given what you have just told me, what are the biggest issues for your department at the moment?"

"I can't recruit to our vacancies, and I can't see how we can continue with our present workload without something dreadful happening," she replied very seriously.

"So what is the real issue that lies behind this?" asked Maxine

"I'm not really sure." said Jill fidgeting in her chair

"So how would you know?" asked Maxine smiling with encouragement.

"I really don't know" replied Jill with a heavy sigh.

"I know you don't know, but if you did know what to do, what might you think the answer would be?" asked Maxine. She had to mask a smile as she

watched Jill attempting to process the question. She was always fascinated at the ease with which these types of questions helped to unlock people when they were stuck in their thinking. She recalled a phrase used frequently by one of her recent teachers. He would say, "You can never solve a problem with the same thinking that created the problem." The types of question she had just asked Jill enabled people to open their minds by creating change in their thinking processes. This in turn enables the creation of solutions.

Suddenly Jill replied, "Well, I could get a overall picture about the people who applied for the job, and why they had turned it down when they were offered the position."

"So how easy would that be to do?" asked Maxine, presupposing that there was an easy solution.

"Well, very easy actually, all I need to do is ask people, and see what happens!" said Jill.

"So when are you going to start collecting that information?" asked Maxine.

"Well, we're interviewing again on Thursday, so I could start it then," said Jill with a big grin.

"Brilliant," said Maxine. "Let's see how Thursday progresses. Come and see me on Friday and we can discuss what you have discovered."

Jill beamed said, "Thank you" and left.

Maxine then looked at her notes, what had she discovered about Jill? She used a lot of visual words so she liked to be able to see where she was going. She also liked details, and had given Maxine so much information about the individual tasks in her department that Maxine had felt almost overwhelmed. She also processed information quite quickly. So given this information, how would she need to manage Jill? I'll need to give her lots of details in order that she can build a bigger picture for herself, and can see where she is going, she thought.

Maxine wrote in her notebook. *Jill – visual, detail orientated -can get bogged down.*

It was almost four o'clock, and time for Maxine's meeting with the Finance and Information Management Director, Richard. I wonder how different he will be she mused as she considered

♦

her meetings with James and Jill.

RICHARD, DIRECTOR OF FINANCE AND INFORMATION

Maxine was brought of her reverie by a knock on the door as Candice came in with a cup of tea, closely followed by Richard who had come prepared with a pile of paperwork. "Oh, before we get started can you just let me have your signature, so that you can sign off our payment runs?" he asked. Maxine looked at him quizzically as he continued. "Everyone is up in arms, as there hasn't been a chief executive for three weeks so no one has been able to sign payments off. Some of our customers are getting very angry."

Maxine swallowed hard and said, "Are you telling me that no payments have been made since my predecessor left?"

"That's right" came the reply.

Maxine was flabbergasted. "So you're telling me that the system is set up so that *only* the chief executive can sign off payments?"

"Yes," he replied, in a very monotone voice.

"Is this honestly what is stated in the Standing Orders and Financial Instructions?" she asked in astonishment.

"Yes," he replied in the same monotone manner.

"Then these need to be changed immediately," said Maxine. "Payments cannot be held up simply because the chief executive is on holiday or away for a few days. We will need to make a recommendation for a change in the Standing Orders and Financial Instructions for our board meeting this month, so

◆

please draft a new recommendation immediately. I'll appreciate the draft for review by the end of this week."

"Well, if you say so, you're the boss," came Richard's rather sardonic reply.

Interesting, thought Maxine. Does this man really relish hierarchy or is this simply a case of sarcasm or passing the buck? "Richard, I also need to know what I'm signing off before I actually sign anything," she said. "So please let me have the support documentation when you leave, and I'll go through this immediately, and call you if I have any queries."

Richard looked a bit bemused, and said "But can't you just sign them now?"

"No, but I'll review them immediately after we've finished our meeting and will have them back to you this evening." She paused for a moment, and then said, "So now that shock is out of the way, please do tell me about your departments and how they operate.'

Once again she listened to what Richard said and how he said things rather than focusing on the content alone. He seemed to be very cautious about what he said. Maxine therefore actively encouraged him by asking, "What are the biggest issues that you're currently facing?"

"The problems in the operations department," he replied.

"What problems specifically?" asked Maxine wanting to clarify any allegations, and check that this was not simply a case of passing responsibility to someone else.

"Well, they keep losing papers, and then take ages to

◆

process things which means we
have delays in our payment runs
or payment dates are missed,"
said Richard.

"So, how long is ages?"
asked Maxine, once again
seeking clarification. She felt that
she really needed to get to the core of the issue.

"Well, we make payment runs on Mondays, and they
say they have too much post on a Monday to be able to get the
paperwork across to us for 2 pm when
we do our payment run."

"Who are 'they'?" asked
Maxine, "and what is the purpose of
having the payment runs on Monday
at 2 pm?" I really have to lift Richard
out of the detail to understand the
overall purpose, if indeed there was
one, she thought. She then noticed that Richard seemed to be
looking very uncomfortable, and started to fidget in his chair.

"Well 'they' are the people in the operations department
and we have always done the payments in this way," he replied.

"But for what purpose has it always been this way?"
asked Maxine as she thought, he seems to be trying to divert
me, however I need to get to the bottom of this, and identify the
overall purpose.

"It fits in with the finance department schedule," he
replied.

◆

"Well, this issue seems to be one of those that's having a fundamental impact on the performance of the organization," said Maxine. "I'm certainly most concerned about delaying any payments unnecessarily. So I'd like you to get together with James, and identify what needs to happen to resolve this matter. The overall focus we need to establish is one of customer care. This means that we need to ensure that we provide our customers with the very best service that we can. We will then discuss your combined proposals at the next Director's meeting in order that we can discuss this as a team, and get other people's ideas," said Maxine.

"What for?" came an astonished reply. "What will other people know about my department that I don't?"

Ouch, thought Maxine as she said, "I think it's important to discuss this with other members of the directors team so that we can be clear about the impact any changes will have on the organization as a whole. I'm also a firm believer in discussing as many ideas as possible to ensure we have the very best solution."

"Oh," he replied looking somewhat perturbed.

Maxine continued, "Tell me Richard how to you assess when you have done a good job?"

"I just know I have," he replied with a bemused expression on his face. Maxine beamed and said, "Ok, thanks Richard. That was very helpful. Please ensure that you get together with James to agree how we can remove this block over the payments. We're having weekly Directors meetings on Mondays so we can discuss your proposals next week. Also let me have the support

♦

documentation to enable me to agree and sign off any payments that are urgent. I'll also ask Candice to set up weekly one to one meetings with you so that we can deal with any departmental issues as they arise."

Richard gulped and said, "Do you really think that's necessary? I've never done this before?"

"Yes, I do think that this is important, and I'd like you to do the same with your team. This will enable everyone to know what they are personally responsible for, and what needs to be done by when. This process makes it really easy to agree to any specific actions needed and to resolve any problems on an ongoing basis."

As he turned to leave, Richard gave Maxine a long look but didn't say anything. Maxine thought, well, he really is an interesting character, so what have I learned about him?

Looking at her notes Maxine realized that Richard was a mismatcher (he will mismatch anyone trying to build rapport, appearing to be argumentative), he was vague and used very non-specific language. Very interesting for a finance director, she thought wryly.

Maxine wrote in her notebook, *Richard – mismatcher, non specific, appears quite defensive, internal validation.*

Candice popped her blonde head around the door, and said, "I'm going home now if that's ok. How was your first day?"

"Very interesting," replied Maxine. "I think I'll make a cup of tea, reflect on what I've learned, and go through the payment schedules before I go home. First thing tomorrow morning will you please find out if we have any comfortable armchairs in the building that I could use in my office? I really need to change the appearance of this office as soon as possible. Also will you get me a copy of the corporate budget statement?"

"I'll do that first thing in the morning," said Candice. "Have a great evening."

"You too," said Maxine. "I'll see you in the morning and thanks for your help today."

As Candice left, Maxine sat in the quiet and reflected on her day. What have I actually learned she mused as she

studied her notes, along with the outline personal profiles of the directors. Well, I'm certainly going to need all of my new skills to turn this place around.

The directors appear to be used to working on their own rather than as a team. They also seem to be doing a lot of hands on work rather than directing. I know that this is a common problem in ailing and low performance organizations, but I actually think I can have great fun turning this around. My goal is to establish a dynamic organization, providing excellent customer services, a place where clients are valued, and know they will receive high quality services. I think I have had a really good first day of discovery. Colin would be intrigued.

Colin had always advised Maxine to use all of the

resources she had available to her. One of his favorite sayings was, "What use is knowledge without experience? It's rather like spending your life in a library full of all the worlds greatest texts and never going out into the world to apply them. The result is you never truly know what works and what doesn't"

Later, as she put on her coat and switched out the light Maxine was thinking, how do I maximize the skills of the people I have in the organization, and what skills do I need to either bring in from elsewhere or train people to develop? With that thought she closed the door on her first day at Extreme Ventures and headed home.

LEARNING POINTS

➤ Stop, look and listen – ask questions to pick up as much intelligence as possible as quickly as possible. Resist the temptation to leap into problem solving mode without all the relevant information.

➤ When you feel yourself getting drawn into 'tick-tock' and the detail, remember to take a deep breath, and stand back to see the big picture.

➤ Place your customers at the heart of the organization. Without your customers there is no organization!

➤ Leading an organization takes a wide range of skills so ensure you have access to personal, external support such as a coach to assist you in developing and honing your skills.

➤ Take short regular breaks in your working day to refresh your energy levels, and keep your thinking fresh.

➤ Identify the types of words people predominately use and then use these types of words when communicating with them, this will help you build rapport. Are they visual (seeing pictures), auditory (hearing the sounds), kinesthetic (getting a feel for what you say) or non-specific (vague and non descriptive)?

➤ To facilitate solution based thinking, ask people to identify at least 3 different solutions to any problem. Only one solution leads to a compulsion, two a dilemma, with three or more you have real choice.

➤ Ask open questions and listen, this will enable you to understand how best to manage someone and the type of support they will need from you.

➤ Create a working environment that is conducive to your style and remove any reminders (anchors) from your predecessor which could hinder performance.

➤ Pay attention to the specific words people use along with their speech patterns (the sequences and types of words). This gives you their operating style and enables you to communicate more effectively with them.

➤ Ask enabling questions to stimulate new ways of thinking. Use When? What? How? questions. Avoid Why? questions to free up thinking.

➤ Use 'specific' questions to identify a core issue and remove any vague generalizations

➤ To lift people out of details, use questions to "chunk up" and obtain the overall purpose or the intention behind an activity or process.

➤ Review your progress at the end of each day and apply all the skills and knowledge you have to increase your daily effectiveness.

3

Identifying the Rules

Maxine awoke early the next morning ready and eager to start her second day. She was aware that she really needed to ensure that she looked after

herself, maintaining her energy, and keeping balanced whilst she undertook this challenging and exciting role. She happily got out of bed, sat quietly, and settled into her usual morning practice of meditation, showered, ate a light breakfast, gave her cat Tosca, his breakfast, kissed her husband goodbye, and set off for Extreme Ventures.

As she drove to the office, Maxine ran through some of the things that she wanted to share with the staff at this morning's meeting. Foremost in her mind was her desire to create an

organization that would be a great place to work, a place where people felt valued, and a place where people were proud to work.

By achieving this she knew that the end result would be an increase in the organization's overall performance. She had heard many new chief executives spout words of wisdom that were politely listened to and then immediately forgotten. She knew that this was her first opportunity to speak to all of the staff together, and a major opportunity to set down new ground rules and ways of working. She also knew that the workforce would be watching her every move.

How do I demonstrate to them that I'm a woman of my word, she thought, as she drove through the morning rush hour traffic. I need to demonstrate that I mean what I say, and say what I mean. They have probably heard lots of platitudes in the past, and need to know that this time it's different, and that they will truly have a say in how the business is run.

So what do I need to do, she asked herself. Well, in my experience it's always the people who are doing the actual work who know how things can be done differently to achieve better results. All they need is a little coaching and support, usually in the form of time to achieve great results. So, if I were a member of staff what would I want to hear from a new chief executive?

I'd want to know that I'm listened to, and that the work that I do is valued. I'd also like to think that I'm considered to be a person rather than just a cog in a mechanistic wheel, and I'd want to enjoy what I do. A comfortable environment to work in would also be good.

Smiling to herself Maxine felt that she had the gist of what she would say, and the culture she wanted to create. She intended to establish a range of task groups across the organization. These groups would comprise of people at all levels throughout the organization, something that is commonly known as diagonal slice groups. Their task will be to identify the best ways to organize and carry out the work of Extreme Ventures. The purpose behind all this work will be to ensure a turn around in organizational performance as quickly as possible.

She heard Colin's voice in her mind say, "The best way to achieve sustainable organizational  change is to involve the staff right from the very outset, to make it *their* organizational change rather than something imposed on them from above."

So Maxine decided that she would get the directors together to brainstorm and identify a number of work streams where performance needed to be improved. She would then ask for volunteers throughout the organization to co-ordinate these groups, and to make recommendations to the Director Management Team for discussion and action. She was very clear that the only prohibitive criterion would be that directors could not be involved in the individual working groups. From what she understood so far, this would be something of a culture shock to an organization, which had a history of hierarchical decision making and imposition.

Well, I must start as I mean to go on, she thought. I need to create an organization that can ultimately function on a day to day basis without the Chief Executive. Then I'll know I've done a great job.

Maxine walked into the office at around 8.30 am, made herself a cup of coffee, and checked her e-mail before the staff meeting. She was amazed to discover that she seemed to be being copied into all sorts of extraneous emails between people who seemed to be moaning at one another.

Who actually takes any action around here, she thought.

She stood up, straightened her skirt suit, took a few deep breaths, and made her way across the hallway to the boardroom. She wanted to arrive a little early so that she could observe people as they arrived for the meeting.

She had been a little perturbed to discover that there were insufficient chairs in the room therefore some people would have to stand up. Is this the first meeting of the entire workforce if there are insufficient chairs for everyone, she asked herself. As people started to arrive, Maxine sensed the low energy, and a general mood of low morale.

These people all look so miserable, she thought. I know this is a mind read on my part, but I haven't seen a single person smile or even acknowledge someone from a different department. They are all sat in their own departmental groups. It looks as if my plans for cross-departmental diagonal slice groups will be quite a challenge.

◆

At 9 o'clock Candice leaned over and whispered, "I think everyone is here."

"Thank you" replied Maxine as she stood up to greet the assembled throng. "Good morning everyone." There were a few murmurings and nods.

"As you're probably aware, I'm Maxine Brown your new chief executive. I haven't yet had the opportunity to meet all of you personally, as this is only my second day in post. However, I do expect to have met everyone by the end of my first month. You're also probably aware that I've been appointed with a specific brief to take Extreme Ventures into the twenty first century, and in order to do this I'm going to need your help."

There seemed to be a look of disbelief on a few faces as if they were thinking, "Did I just hear her say that she wants our help?" As she spoke part of Maxine's attention was focusing on

identifying who were the rapport group leaders within the organization. Whilst they may not hold positions of formal authority within an organization, they are the people of influence who lead groups of people by their unconscious ability to build rapport. She knew that she would need to consciously build rapport with these people as quickly as possible if her plans to develop and turn the organization around were to be successful.

"I know the company has been through some difficult times recently, and I'm very keen that we work together to put in place new systems and procedures that will help you to do your jobs effectively, and to enjoy doing this at the same time. Therefore I'm going to ask for volunteers to help me with this challenging task. Those of you who are working within the departments will know far better than I will, what does and does not work. You're the experts."

Maxine could see that she was grabbing the attention of a number of people, and had quickly identified about six rapport group leaders. As usual these were not necessarily the more senior people.

I must find out from Candice who these people are and what their roles are in the organization, she thought. She carefully made a mental note of where these people were sitting and what they were wearing.

"It's my intention to set up a number of task groups to identify where we can make changes to put our customers at the heart of our organization. These groups will also look at how working conditions can be improved, and how we can increase the overall performance of Extreme Ventures. I'll send an email out later today identifying the groups, and asking for volunteers to lead and participate in these. Each group will be given time to work through the issues and to make recommendations to the Directors Management Team at the end of the month.

"I really want to know what is important to you as employees of Extreme Ventures, so I'm very keen to listen to

◆

people's ideas. You will soon discover that I value openness and honesty above all else, I want to know what works really well and what gets in the way. I also want to hear about ideas to engage our customers in this process, and to make this a fun and exciting place to work. You should also know that I operate an open door policy. This literally means when my door is physically open I'm happy to meet with anyone who feels that they have something important to share, so if you have a good idea I want to know about it."

She smiled and said, "I know many of you may think you have heard this kind of thing before but I want you to know that I'm really committed to turning this organization around, and I want us to do it together.

"I'm really looking forward to working with you all."

There was a small ripple of applause from a group of people at the back of the room. With this Maxine smiled and headed back to her office. There was a silent lull, and then she heard the inevitable chatter as she walked through her office door. She grinned wryly, thinking, I hope I have stirred something up there.

Maxine had indicated to the directors that she would like a brief word with them, so they had followed behind her into her office. "I'd like your thoughts on the groups we should set up," she said. "There appear to be some key areas that I know we need to look at such as customer services, but what are your thoughts?"

Richard looked at her and said, "Well, finance is fine, nothing needs to change there."

◆

An interesting initial response, thought Maxine as she replied, "Richard, things may be organized well in finance but this provides a wonderful opportunity to test out new ideas, and to hear what staff throughout the organization really think. I'd like you all to think about areas for improvement and to talk to your teams about any ideas they have."

"I know we need to look at how the operations and finance departments could work more effectively together," chirped in James. "Richard said you had mentioned that you wanted us to do this, and I think it's important. From what you have just said Maxine, I think it will be great to involve the key members of staff in this. So I think this should be one of the working groups."

"Great," said Maxine "So what shall we call it?"

"An operations and finance working group" volunteered James.

"Good idea," said Maxine, encouraging James. "But to give the group members a more specific steer I think the group title needs to be more specific." Here is another example of wooly thinking she thought then said, "So, what would be the purpose of their work?"

"To improve the processing of customer claims," said James.

"Yes, and what is the purpose of this?" asked Maxine as she used specific questions to 'chunk-up' the thinking.

"To increase our efficiency, setting a standard processing time," he replied.

"Excellent," encouraged Maxine. "And what would be the purpose of that?"

"To have happy customers," he said with a grin.

"Yes, the whole purpose of this change process is to have happy customers, because happy customers refer other customers, and so increase our business. Great work," said Maxine. "So which other areas would benefit from review?"

"Can you tell us a little more about your views about our customers and customer service?" asked Jill rather tentatively.

"Well, as I've mentioned before we need to place our customers at the center of Extreme Ventures activity. Without our customers, we're not in business. So for me there's a need to identify how best this can be achieved,' replied Maxine. 'Consequently, what other groups do you think we should have?"

Within twenty minutes they had brainstormed a range of ideas and identified specific working groups:

*   The specific action required ensuring that customers are placed at the center of the Extreme Ventures agenda, including the identification of standards to increase the efficiency of processing customer claims.

- The identification of targets to improve the efficiency and accuracy of processing customer claims.
- The identification of the changes required to maximize the use of facilities (internal and external), and work space.
- The identification of the specific support services required for all Extreme Ventures activities.
- The identification of key changes and actions to improve efficiency within the Operations Department.
- The identification of key changes and actions to improve efficiency within the Contracting Department.
- The identification of standards to increase the efficiency of processing customer claims.
- The development and implementation of key performance indicators throughout Extreme Ventures.
- The key issues to be included in the annual business plan and development program.
- The identification of opportunities for additional income generation.

As the directors left Maxine said, "Richard will you please check with your team that they do not wish to review any of their specific activities. I want to make sure they have the same opportunities as everyone else." Richard glanced backwards with a seemingly reluctant cursory nod.

Maxine mulled the session over in her mind; Jill and James had really seemed to enjoy the brief brainstorming process. Richard however had appeared to be very ill at ease. She knew from past experience that forcing people to participate ran

◆

counter to effective change management. I need to remember to avoid bulldozing people at this early stage, she thought. So, if finance does not want to play at this stage, that's fine. They may change their minds though when they see that I really mean what I say. She paused, thinking, yes, only time will tell.

Maxine sat down and drafted an email to send to all the staff asking for volunteers to join the various task groups, setting out the brief and timescales for reporting their recommendations. The thinking in the organization seemed to be so waffly that she thought some very direct instructions would be needed to ensure the success of the work.

I'll ask for a response by the end of the week in order that we can get the groups established early next week, she thought, and then Candice can collate all of the responses.

After sending out the email Maxine got up and went into the outer office where Candice was sat at her desk. "Candice, how far have you got with arranging for me to meet some of our customers?" she enquired.

"It has been really funny," said Candice. "One of them, Joshua Wainwright at Pipeline said, 'You mean the Chief Executive wants to know what we think? And she wants to come and meet me here? After all this time I can't believe anyone at Extreme Ventures cares about their customers. This I have to see – do tell her that it won't be very pretty."

◆

"Great," said Maxine. "He sounds just the type of customer I need to meet. When am I meeting him?"

"Tomorrow morning at 11.00, he has cleared his diary to meet with you."

"Excellent," said Maxine. "This should be very revealing, I really am looking forward to meeting him."

The next morning Maxine drove across town to meet with Joshua Wainwright. She was really keen to understand Extreme Ventures customer base, and what they really felt about the services provided by Extreme Ventures as a company. Her goal was to listen and then demonstrate that she was committed to creating genuine relationships with customers, turning Extreme Ventures into an organization that listened and delivered. As Maxine soon discovered Joshua was frank and open, attempting to get her to rise to any bait he threw out.

His introductory remarks were, "Well, I just had to meet

the poor soul who took over Extreme Ventures. You're either very stupid or very bright, and I suppose time will tell the full story."

Maxine had smiled and replied somewhat tongue in cheek, "Well, I'm really pleased to meet you too, I can see we're going to have a lively conversation. Perhaps you could start by telling me about the problems you have been experiencing with Extreme Ventures and what you would like us to do instead."

"Well remember," he said. "You asked for it." Then with a wicked grin he launched into a long list of problems and unsatisfactory experiences. Maxine spent almost an hour listening to Joshua's list of issues and the way he felt they should be tackled.

At the end of the meeting she asked, "Considering all the problems you have experienced with Extreme Ventures, why did you keep sending us your business?"

"Quite frankly," he replied. "There are no other companies in the area who can do this work for us, otherwise we would have moved our business months or even years ago!"

Maxine thanked Joshua for his frankness, and said she would call him in the next four weeks to discuss the impact of the changes they would be implementing.

I really need to get some early wins with the customers if the service he has been receiving is typical. I hope it isn't, but I get the sense that it probably is, she thought somewhat wistfully.

Maxine spent the rest of her first week talking to and visiting customers as well as getting to know the people who

◆

worked at Extreme Ventures. The messages from the customers appeared to be consistent. No one seemed to listen to them, and they could not get through to people on the phone. When they finally did, they were continually frustrated that the promised return calls, were never forthcoming. In fact, it was a litany of 'the worst possible ways to treat customers'. Having heard all of the issues, she was surprised that Extreme Ventures had any customers at all.

During this first week the staff at Extreme Ventures were slowly getting used to the fact that on her way in each morning Maxine would pop into one of the departments to seek some advice from someone, or simply to discuss something about how things worked or not. Some people still viewed her with suspicion but thankfully others were beginning to open up. The finance and information teams were the ones who really seemed to find this all a bit strange. So much so, that one day Richard had asked her why she talked to his staff rather than going to him first.

"Because I like to test the temperature of the organization directly from time to time," she said. "Without the sanitization of a third party."

He had mumbled to himself, and disappeared back into is office. Richard and I are going to have some interesting times, thought Maxine as she walked back to her office. It will be fascinating to see how things pan out over the next few weeks.

On Friday afternoon Maxine sat in her office, reflecting on her progress so far. She noted down her achievements, and reviewed her goals. She was certain that she had some good

people with real potential working in Extreme Ventures. The problem seemed to be that their identity and self worth had simply been eroded by constant problems with little means of support to resolve them.

She had managed to change the ambience of her office by removing the big heavy furniture, and introducing a coffee table and armchairs. These had been found in a storage cupboard where they had never been unpacked. Next week a smaller desk and chair was arriving, so she would have much more space which would further reduce the oppressiveness.

I'll buy a few pictures with inspirational quotes to brighten up the walls next week and to complete the revamp, she said to herself. It's finally beginning to feel like a pleasant space to work in. I'm pleased that I can actually go home feeling that I'm making progress, real progress.

The hill I have to climb may be steep, and I know there will be a few boulders to encounter on the way, but that's all part of joy of leading an organization.

◆

As she walked out of the office that evening Maxine knew in her heart that she had made the right decision when she agreed to take up the position of chief executive. She climbed into her car, switched on her CD player, and started to listen to a track by Labi Sifri, *Something Inside So Strong*. As she pulled out of the car park she felt that the lyrics were written just for her at this very moment in time.

◆

LEARNING POINTS

➤ Keep your life in balance by undertaking
a daily practice such as meditation,
or spending a few minutes in nature to
ground your energy.

➤ Set clear ground rules and ways of
working from the outset.

➤ Mean what you say and say what you mean.
As Ghandi said, 'Be the change you
seek in the world'. Forget platitudes
and be congruent with what you say.

➤ Engage as many people as possible in
your vision, right from the outset. Listen to
what people have to say, regardless of their
position and engage them in reshaping 'their'
organization, and truly value their contributions.

➤ Get to know who people are and what they
do. Get out of your office and ask questions.

➤ Identify the organization's rapport group
leaders. They can assist you in building
rapport with more people in your
organization quickly and easily.

➤ Establish time limited task groups to tackle specific organizational problems.

➤ Engage those who want to be engaged in shaping the organization. Forcing participation will result in resentment and dilution of the overall process.

➤ Find out what customers really want and take any appropriate action. Be honest and keep them informed of any changes.

➤ Take time to set your goals, and review your progress daily and weekly. This provides focus, and allows corrections to be made when necessary.

Part 2 – Going Barefoot

4

Engaging the Team

Maxine was looking forward to her coaching session with Colin. She had now been at Extreme Ventures for almost three weeks, and had begun to make real progress in understanding the culture of the organization, and in uncovering the entrenched ideas and attitudes of some members of staff. The 'diagonal slice' working groups really seemed to be making a difference to morale with people actually looking alive, motivated and determined to succeed as their new ideas evolved.

Candice who was a part of one of the groups and a bit of a mole for Maxine said that someone in her group had said, "This is really great fun, I can see how we can really alter things

around here. But do you really think that Miss Brown, err... Maxine will listen to what we have to say? Or do you think this is just a fancy exercise in PR?"

When she heard this Maxine thought, I need to remember to ensure that I give regular honest feedback on a consistent basis. If we cannot do something I need to ensure I explain why. Too many people have been ignored for far too long, my most important job as ever is about effective communication. The challenge right now is coaching the rest of the top team to do the same. How? Well, this is something ideal to discuss with Colin.

As Maxine pulled her car into the driveway of Colin's office, memories of her first visit about 6 months ago flooded into her mind. She had known that she needed to change something in her life and career, and had felt at a complete crossroads, not knowing which way to turn. Now six months on, here she was a new chief executive with her very own organization to grow and develop. Her energy levels when she first came to see Colin had been very low, she had felt like she was going through the motions of life rather than really living life to the full. In most people's eyes, she was a successful contented woman with a good career and great relationship with her husband. She knew however that she was in a rut, and in her heart, she felt that something was missing. She had been discussing this with Jan one of her very good friends and a valued colleague. Jan had suggested that Maxine would probably benefit from spending some time with a professional coach to help put her back on track.

Jan had said, "You know Maxine I think I know

◆

someone who could really help you. His name is Colin, and he is a professional coach. I had a series of coaching sessions with him recently and it really made a difference to my life and work. He certainly helped me to see things in a very different way. I now have more energy to do the things I truly want to do, and I also enjoy myself a lot more. I would recommend him to anyone who really wants to succeed or has got stuck, and needs a helping hand to become unstuck. He taught me how easy it is to be in control even at the most difficult times.

"Most of the successful people I know have an excellent coach, they swear by them, and I have to say I wouldn't be able to do half of the things I do now if it had not been for Colin. Give it a go, what have you got to lose?"

Now Maxine knew exactly what Jan had meant all those months ago. It already seemed like another lifetime.

She reflected and thought, looking back, that was a conversation that really changed my life.

As she rang the doorbell Maxine knew she would be leaving her coaching session more focused, and with more useful tools to turn Extreme Ventures into a successful vibrant organization. The door opened to reveal the warm, friendly,

◆

smiling face of Colin. He always seemed so alive with his shock of white hair highlighting his twinkling deep brown eyes.

"So how is the new chief executive?" he enquired grinning from ear to ear as he gave her a big bear hug, "It's so good to see you."

"I'm absolutely great, Colin, but also a little tired," Maxine replied. "I know I have a number of challenges ahead, but I can see them as opportunities to learn from so that I can become a really effective chief executive."

"Excellent," responded Colin. "Come on in, and lets see what we can do today to move things on even further."

Maxine had come prepared with a list of issues to discuss with Colin. She knew from experience that he was always very careful to identify the desired outcomes for the session right at the outset. She also knew that he would always ensure that these were achieved or if not, ways in which they could be achieved.

As they settled into

the comfy chairs in Colin's coaching room they sipped some delicious freshly made hot coffee, and munched some home made chocolate chip cookies.

Colin asked, "So what do you want to achieve during our time together today?"

"I've identified seven key issues, some of which seem to interrelate," replied Maxine. "Shall I list them?"

Colin nodded, and Maxine began to read out her list, "First of all I want to be able to develop the top team to increase their individual and collective performance.

Secondly, I really need to engage our customers effectively and to gain their confidence. Thirdly, I want to explore what to do about the two or three people who do not want to participate in the change process. Then, I'd like to share what I've discovered, and my learnings so far to make sure I've maximized these. And, fifthly, how do I combine bottom up with top down thinking?

"I think the final two link in with the rest in some way – morale, and investing in people and the working environment."

"OK," said Colin. "So, given the time we have to spend together today, which of the issues you have identified is the most important?"

Maxine grinned, "It doesn't matter how specific or prepared I think I am," she said. "You always demonstrate to me that I need to be even clearer in my thinking. I have no doubt that the most important is the potential stumbling blocks. Hopefully they are not as large as I seem to think they are. Then it will be really good to discuss the development of the top team. Is that ok?"

"Excellent," replied Colin. "So let us start by you telling me what you have discovered so far, and describe to me these so called stumbling blocks."

Maxine took out her notebook, and spent about fifteen minutes describing all that she had discovered about Extreme Ventures, the issues with staff and

customer morale, and all the steps that she had taken so far to raise the energy of the organization to start to move the whole thing forward. Colin sat and listened, taking a few notes from time to time, and only asking questions to seek clarification.

It feels so good to be really listened to, thought Maxine. She concluded by saying, "The issues seem to be as follows;

1. What do I do about the finance team and Richard's leadership of them? He seems to be very defensive and resistant to anything he perceives as stepping on his territory. Is it important that the whole organization joins in or not? Is it ok for the finance and information teams to opt out at this stage?

2. How do I keep the momentum of the change process going, and sustain the enthusiasm that I seem to have initiated by these 'diagonal slice' workshops in the longer term? They have had such a positive impact on morale that I really want to build on this and keep the energy of the organization high.

◆

3. How do I best keep the customers engaged whilst we go through all of this change? I know I have a brief 'honeymoon period' with them and I really want to make sure I engage them for the longer term.

4. How do I develop a top team that delivers, and what about any casualties?

5. How do I keep myself sane through all of this?"

Colin laughed and said, "You really have been having fun haven't you? In order to make sense of all of this let's take one issue at a time as each of the first four issues you raise link well into what you say you want to achieve in our time together today. In order to maximize the impact of these, let's start with your second and third points, which are really about sustained cultural change. Is that ok with you?"

"Absolutely," replied Maxine. "I rather blurted everything out didn't I? It just feels such a relief to share all of this with someone. Tom, my husband is great about it, but there's a limit to how much I want to drag my work life into my home life."

Colin nodded and said, "You say that you have identified six rapport group leaders across the organization. Are they spread across the organization? And in particular is there someone in the finance department?"

"Yes, and yes," replied Maxine.

"Great," said Colin. "So, given what you have learned about the organization so far and your long term vision, combined with the fact that you have at least one group rapport leader in each department, what do you now need to do?"

"I'm really not sure," replied Maxine.

"I know you're not sure, but if you were sure what might some of the options be?" asked Colin, knowing that this question was the type of question that would unblock Maxine's stuck thinking, and enable her mind to identify new possibilities along with some possible options.

"Well, I need to ensure I have some kind of long term relationship with the rapport group leaders that will enable me to maintain rapport with the people throughout the organization. I just don't know what to do about the

rapport mismatchers," she replied. "Let's leave them to one side for now," said Colin. "and focus on maximizing your overall leverage. Do you recall the hundredth monkey syndrome research?"

"I don't think I've even heard of that one," replied Maxine furrowing her brow.

Colin nodded in acknowledgement, and continued, "Some years ago there were a group of Japanese research scientists on a cluster of remote pacific islands. I'm not sure exactly what purpose of their research was, but they discovered something quite phenomenal. They flew over these islands every few days, and dropped some sweet potatoes on the beach for the local resident monkeys to eat. Occasionally a sweet potato would land in the ocean. One day they noticed a female monkey

◆

take her potato into the ocean to wash the sand off. She did this for a number of days and clearly enjoyed her 'sand – free' potato. After a few occasions, one or two of the other younger monkeys modeled her and also took their potatoes into the ocean to wash the sand off. Then others gradually began to follow suit. As if by magic, there came a point when *all* of the monkeys on *all* of the nearby islands went into the ocean, and swashed the sand off their potatoes before eating them. The trigger to this seemed to be when ten percent of the monkeys went into the water to wash their potatoes the rest automatically adopted the same behavior. The hundredth

monkey research demonstrated that ten percent of the population triggers the remaining ninety percent to adopt the same behavior. What is so phenomenal is that, regardless of the fact that there had been no direct physical contact between the monkeys on the various islands, they all developed the same behavior."

"Wow," said Maxine. "So does that mean that I only need to have ten percent of people aligned to the new culture and the rest will naturally follow?"

"That's absolutely correct," replied Colin.

"Is it really that simple?" asked Maxine. "What about the famous mismatchers?"

"Yes it is, that simple. Tell me, what do you mean by a mismatcher Maxine?"

"He or she is someone who appears to constantly disagree with the people they are communicating with. This often results in arguments and people getting fed up with being contradicted all the time. It really disrupts meetings, and often other people do not want to work with the 'mismatcher'."

"Precisely, so given this, what is the best way to manage and communicate with these people?" Colin enquired.

"Well, would it be to mismatch them?" she asked tentatively. "Although if that's the case, it would feel really 'odd'."

"Yes that is precisely the case, and how do you think you could do this in an organizational context, given what you know about people's preferences for communicating?"

"I need to find a mismatching task for them to do," she replied.

Colin once again smiled and nodded as he asked, "Such as?"

"Ah ha, the light is dawning," exclaimed Maxine. "I need to task them with something that will be beneficial for us all, and that they will feel is worthwhile. Would it work if I asked them to let us know when things were going off track or to identify any pitfalls?"

"What do you think?" asked Colin, grinning at how his

◆

young coachee was creating new possibilities and solutions.

"Yes, it will work," she blurted out. " I could ask Richard to tell us when we're at risk. He would really enjoy that. Ah, but then, how do I stop him from being destructive?"

"When would be the most productive time to know about potential problems?" asked Colin.

"When we've formulated the ideas and yet prior to implementation. Yes, that's it, he can focus on listening whilst we're in creative mode, and then assess the risk once we think we have ideas formed into actions and outcomes. How brilliant! All I need to do is agree some principles with him, it sounds so simple."

"Aren't all the best solutions? It goes back to the old adage of KISS. (Keep It Simple Stupid). Too many people try to complicate things because they think they need to. When in actual fact the best results are the simplest and easiest to implement," said Colin with a grin.

Maxine reflected for a moment or two, and then said, "I suppose now I think about it, all the great leaders I've admired have kept things simple."

Colin's eyes twinkled as he nodded and said, "So lets get to the nub of all of this, which seems to me to be about creating an organizational strategy that defines the culture and direction of travel. Does one currently exist?"

"I was told at my interview that there was one but I've seen no evidence of its existence," she replied. "Anyway, I think it would be good to create something new and vibrant that represents a dynamic customer focused organization. The only thing is, I'm just not sure how best to go about it. But what I do know is that I need to engage people, the uncertainty is about who and at what stage."

"Where and who do you think the direction needs to come from?" asked Colin.

"I think it's probably two places," said Maxine. "It's important that the top of the organization demonstrates overall leadership, but I also think it needs to come from the people who work throughout the organization not just the directors and board members."

"So how do you envisage the 'diagonal slice' working groups you have set up feeding into this?" asked Colin.

Maxine mulled this over before saying, "I hadn't actually, but your question has prompted me to think that it could and should. The groups are currently feeding back on how to tackle specific issues that get in the way of the company delivering it's core business as current practice defines. They are also identifying a range of ideas for future developments in each of the key areas."

◆

"Great," said Colin. "So what will be the best way to build on these?"

"What do you think about me using these to inform a workshop for the board? I know we need to spend some time looking ahead and identifying where we want to position Extreme Ventures in the market. I really think it will help the board members to understand the basic building blocks of the business, and to then create a vision for now and the future based on a combined 'top–down', 'bottom–up' approach. Mmmmm, that sounds really great. But how can I also engage the customers in this? They have had such a raw deal, and it would be great if they could become real partners rather than people and organizations who are 'done to'."

"Using the recommendations from the working groups is a great way to create the vision if you combine this with the top-down, bottom-up approach you describe. As far as the customers go, how is the group looking at customer services approaching their task?" queried Colin.

"Actually they have developed a structured questionnaire that they have e-mailed to all of our customers, and they will have interviewed about ten percent face to face. Hence, in the

next week or two, they will have an idea about the key issues. Perhaps we can then invite our customers to a short workshop. We could then ask their views about our vision and organizational strategy when it's in draft format, and then we can get their direct feedback.

"Hey, I really like that idea. We could also have an open day and introduce them to key people, who we could designate as their personal customer account contact. In this way they will have a face to go with the name. Colin, this is really great. I'm feeling better and better every minute," Maxine responded as a broad smile swept across her face.

"Great,' replied Colin. "Do you have any more questions about establishing the overall culture of the company? Or are we done?"

"Well, actually, yes I do have one," said Maxine. "How do I keep all of this alive and vibrant?"

"Ok, what usually keeps an organization vibrant in your experience?" Colin gently countered.

"Well," she replied. "It's the chief executive and his, or her team. They are usually very visible and accessible, and have a good strong leadership style which includes really listening to people within the organization. They also continually challenge these people to grow and develop. They have a good sense of the 'organizational thermometer', the hot spots and challenges within the organization, and they are also consistently ahead of the game."

"So how do you ensure you do this?" Colin asked.

"Well, I'll ensure I'm visible and accessible which I think

◆

I've already started, I simply need to ensure that I continue to do

this. I also talk to people directly, and am genuinely interested in what they are doing, and how this fits within the overall business of the organization. So I need to ensure that they know this, and they are clear about how their specific roles fit into the business of Extreme Ventures," Maxine stated.

Colin nodded his agreement and said, " I think we've made great progress today Maxine. Is there anything else we need to discuss about this?"

"Well, my brain is buzzing and feeling alive with new thoughts," she replied.

"That sounds good to me," said Colin. "We now both need to be sure that we're clear about what actions or steps you're holding yourself accountable for. So, what are you agreeing to do by when?'"

"Ok, first of all, I'll ensure I pop into each department at least once a week to check the organizational thermometer and to pick up any soft intelligence. I'll talk directly to individual people to see how they feel about the changes and what else we

◆

could be doing to improve performance or working conditions.

"We will develop an organizational strategy and outline business plan by the end of next month that clearly sets out the strategic direction and organizational goals for the year. I'll then have regular monthly staff briefings about progress, and ensure that directors talk this through with their teams so that everyone knows where their role and activities fits within the overall plan.

"Thirdly, I'll ask for direct feedback from the staff about how real and alive they think the plan is in relation to their own work. We will then review this in six months time."

"Excellent stuff," said Colin. "We will check your progress at our next coaching session. So let's move on, what do you need to do to develop your top team?"

"Well, given the various abilities, obvious strengths and weaknesses of the team members, and their lack of cross directorate working, I'm unsure about how I can build a cohesive dynamic and vibrant team to lead the organization."

"Have I told you one of my pet phrases?" asked Colin.

"I'm not sure," she responded.

"Well, the one I'm thinking of is 'Different strokes for different folks'" he said.

Maxine looked somewhat

bemused as she toyed with the words in her mind.

"Let me remind you" said Colin, rising to draw on the flip chart. "We discussed this in one of our early sessions together. It's adapted from a model developed by Max Landsberg, and discussed in his book, *The Tao of Coaching*. There are two key issues to be addressed when managing people. The first is their skill and the second their motivation. Some people will demonstrate low skills and little motivation, hence they will need to be directed in a very hands-on way. Other people will be highly motivated and highly skilled, you can delegate to these people in the knowledge that they will deliver, and if they can't you can rest assured that they will discuss this with you. Another group are those who are highly motivated, and yet, have little of the required skills, these people you will need to guide. Others

will be highly skilled and yet have little motivation, you will need to enthuse and get these people excited to enable them to become motivated to deliver. In summary here are the types and ways to enable them to deliver," said Colin.

"Direct those who have little motivation and poor skills by being very specific about what is required with clear timescales. Identify what motivates them and train them to acquire the skills. These people require close supervision until they become more able, then you can relax control as they demonstrate improvement in performance. If required you may

◆

need to tighten control again from time to time, and as they learn and progress you can release the control once more.

"Guide those who have few skills and yet are highly motivated. They will need you to explain things to them, and to answer their questions. You in turn will need to allow a few early mistakes and create the environment to learn from these and move on.

"Enthuse those who are highly skilled, and yet show little motivation. Identify the reasons for their lack of motivation, and find ways to assist them in overcoming these.

"The whole idea is to move people to a place of delegation where you can simply coach them from time to time and create the environment to enable them to do the job. All you will need to do then is to set clear objectives and outcomes, and allow them to develop their own ways of doing this. You can also involve them in decision-making and ask their opinions. Remember to stretch them, and adopt a very 'hands off' management style."

'Wow,' said Maxine. 'I can see how my top team fits into each of these categories. James the Director of Operations has low motivation and low skills, so he needs directing, whereas Jill is highly motivated but hasn't been trained, so needs more guidance from me at this point in time. Now as for Richard, the Director of Finance, I know he has little motivation but what I don't know yet if he is highly skilled or not, he is so very secretive and non-participatory, so he could need either directing or enthusing. Candice my PA, she is both highly motivated and highly skilled. Thank goodness I have someone I can delegate to even if she is the most junior of them all. Colin this is really

◆

helpful stuff."

Colin's eyes twinkled in delight as Maxine continued, "So returning to Richard and the Finance team, it looks as if I need to identify whether he really has the skills or not. I can test this shortly as he needs to prepare the final accounts by the end of next month. This will be a good test of his true abilities along with the work on organizational costings that I've asked him to do. In the meantime, I'll simply keep building the relationships with people in his department" Maxine said with a sigh. "I'll also be interested to see how he reacts to the outcome of the diagonal slice group that's looking at the tasks that interface between the operations and finance departments.

"Colin, once the reports are in from the 'diagonal slice' groups, do you think it would be a good idea to organize a session with the board to clarify the organizational direction? This could then be used as the vehicle to establish an organizational strategy and an annual business plan."
"What specifically were you thinking of?" asked Colin.

'Well, I'd want it to be a highly creative session where we can do some clear blue sky thinking, whilst also undertaking some team building. I know that they have never done anything like this before, and I'd like to be a part of that process rather than leading it. In order to do this I know we will need some external help. It really needs to be someone who can operate at a board level, and have all the skills to move us through some potentially tricky discussions. I'm also finding it challenging to lift the board into strategic mode as they love the details so much, so some help in doing this will be invaluable."

Colin smiled, "This is often the case when an organization has been in crisis or experienced difficulties, people drop back into roles that are comfortable to them. This tends to be operational and as  we know the thinking that created the problem cannot solve the problem. So some fresh thinking and positive challenges are what are called for. It can be handled very effectively by setting a simple agenda; this will enable people to think about things in new and different ways."

"It sounds to me as if we could do with your expertise and help Colin," said Maxine. "Is this something you would be willing to help us with?"

"Of course. I'll be delighted to help. How would you like me to assist?"

"I'd love it if you would help me to design the day and then run it for me. I know they will respond positively to your wisdom and gravitas. Also, I'd then have the confidence to sit back and participate in the day as a member of the team."

"Ok," said Colin. "This sounds good, so lets be clear about outcomes, and keep the session simple and effective. A key focus could be about where Extreme Ventures wishes to be in five years time, and then the steps to get you there. From this we will be able to shape a vision to establish the type of organization Extreme Ventures will become, and how to effectively engage it's customers and staff. Does that sounds like a plan?"

"Brilliant!" exclaimed Maxine. "Can we possibly set a date in the next six weeks?"

"Of course," replied Colin. "Let's do this before you leave today as this seems to bring us nicely to your last point, which was about how to keep your energy up whilst all of this is going on. What are you currently doing to keep yourself balanced or sane as you put it?"

"I'm meditating daily. Well, most days if I'm honest, but

that doesn't seem to be enough."

"So, what about regular exercise? And are you eating a balanced diet? How are you looking after yourself mentally, emotionally and physically?" Colin enquired with a compassionate look on his face.

◆

Maxine squirmed in her seat. "Ok, I get the message, in fact, I realize I haven't really been exercising at all not even at the weekends. Tom is also starting to say I don't seem very enthusiastic about doing anything with him in the evenings either. Hmmm.... I had better sort this one out hadn't I?"

"So, what will you commit yourself to do?" asked Colin with a quirky grin.

"Let me see, ok, I commit myself to swimming three times a week and listening to my husband so that we plan relaxation times together especially at the weekends. In fact, I'll book us into that lovely farmhouse we like to go to in California where we can have long walks on the beach, have a daily massage, and use the Jacuzzi.' She paused, "Hmmm, thanks Colin I needed that reminder. It seems so easy for me to forget to look after myself!"

"Well, I'm glad we got that one sorted, because if you

I WILL **DO** WHAT I **SAY** I WILL **DO**!

don't look after yourself who else will? And if you're out of balance how can you lead your organization effectively?" said Colin with a cheeky smile.

"Ok, point taken," mumbled Maxine sheepishly.

Colin smiled again and asked, "Well, I think we've covered all that you said you wanted to cover. Are we done or have we missed anything?"

"No, I think we're done," said Maxine.

◆

"I have plenty to go away and do!"

"Ok, so all we need to do now is to review the things you said you will do, set a date to follow these up, and set a date for your board session," said Colin. He paused to check he had agreement to this and then said, "So what are you going to do and by when?"

Maxine ran through her action list and said, "This feels great I know what I need to do and when to do it by. I feel much more on-purpose and that's great. Thank you."

"Well done," said Colin. "As ever, I look forward to hearing about your progress."

LEARNING POINTS

➤ Give honest and regular feedback on a consistent basis. If something cannot be done explain why, rather than simply dismissing an idea.

➤ Find yourself a coach, someone who will support you, and also challenge you to 'be more' while attaining and maintaining a balanced life.

➤ At the beginning of any process, set clear measurable outcomes. This enables you to know when you have actually achieved your goals.

➤ List your priorities for a day or task (a maximum of seven). Prioritize these, then 'do' number one until it's complete or can be passed to someone else and then move to your second priority and repeat working your way through your list.

➤ To really understand someone practice 'real listening'. Pay full attention to what they are saying and clear your head of any other thoughts, keep focused on what they are saying and ask questions only to clarify meaning. Otherwise keep quiet. Once you can do this you will truly hear what someone is saying.

➤ Use specific questioning to assist people in freeing up their thinking. Remember the same thinking that created a problem cannot find the solution. Effective questioning facilitates people in becoming unstuck.

➤ Cultural change takes place once 10% of a population changes their behavior. (100th Monkey Syndrome)

➤ Build rapport with 'mismatchers' by mismatching them. Mismatchers are very valuable to an organization if given appropriate roles.

➤ Keep things simple (KISS – keep it simple stupid!)

➤ A sustainable organization combines both a top-down and bottom up approach.

➤ Customers are fundamental to any business, so identify what they want and use this to inform your business strategy.

➤ Listen to what your staff have to say, get to know people by name and as a person rather than just a cog in an organizational wheel. Acknowledge their contribution to the overall business.

➤ When managing a team or group of people remember, "Different strokes for different folks!"

➤ Direct people with little motivation and poor skills; Guide people with few skills who are highly motivated; Enthuse people who are highly skilled with little motivation

➤ Team building starts at the very top of an organization. This facilitates the establishment of a corporate style to ensure everyone is traveling in the same direction.

➤ Look after yourself by keeping yourself in good shape mentally, emotionally and physically. Balance across these three aspects is fundamental to success and sustainability.

➤ Hold yourself (and others) to account to do the things you say that you will do. This gives a clear message that you mean what you say and say what you do – key aspects of sustainable success.

5

Creating the Win-Win

The next morning Maxine was at her desk feeling that she now had a clear direction and focus to enable her to start moving Extreme Ventures forward. Honoring her commitment to her well-being, she had called into the local pool for an early swim on her way into the office. She smiled to herself as she recalled she had forgotten over the last few weeks how invigorating and energizing swimming was. She realized that she found swimming up and down the pool to be like a moving meditation. She would ask herself a question and then focus on her body as it moved through the water. After completing her 25 laps, her mind was clear, and she had the solutions she was looking for. This morning she had been forming her action plan following her coaching session with Colin, and could now see what she needed to do to forge ahead.

Maxine started to review her action list:

- Pop into each department at least once a week to check the organizational thermometer, and to pick up any soft intelligence.
- Talk to Brian (the chairman) about the board strategy development session with Colin.
- Use the outcomes of the diagonal slice work groups to develop the business plan within the context of the organizational strategy.
- Arrange an open day for customers to receive informal feedback, and establish personal customer account contacts (named people to handle specific client accounts).
- Arrange a half-day workshop with willing customers to identify the level of service they would like from Extreme Ventures, and get their feedback on the overall strategic direction of the organization.
- Direct James; guide Jill; delegate to Candice, and task Richard with identifying key areas of organizational risk.

This should also identify the level of input required from me and should satisfy Richard's mismatching tendencies, she thought.

Maxine reviewed her list and then asked herself which of these 6 tasks was the most important. She decided it was the board strategy day, as this would set the overall organizational direction. Next, she would ask Candice to collate the outcomes of the diagonal slice working groups to feed into this workshop. A customer workshop also needed to be scheduled and organized

◆

about two weeks prior to the board development day. This would enable the outcomes of the customer workshop to be fed into the board development session facilitated by Colin. Furthermore a customer open day would be scheduled after the board workshop so that the ideas developed could be commented on directly by the customers. The remaining two tasks were ongoing, providing the appropriate level of support to the directors and Candice, and her regular checks of the organizational thermometer. Maxine sighed as she leaned back in her chair and reviewed her list:

1. Schedule and discuss board strategy day with Brian; draft brief.
2. Ask Candice to collate the outcomes of diagonal slice groups for me to review.
3. Schedule workshop for customers to feed ideas into board strategy day.
4. Schedule a customer open day to test ideas for corporate strategy for the board workshop. Send out invitations.
5. Identify and provide appropriate levels of support for directors.
6. Create time to check the "organizational thermometer".

   Great, she thought. I really can deliver on these quickly and easily.

   She walked over to her office door, and saw that Candice was already sat at her desk reviewing her emails.

   "Good morning, Candice," she said. "When you have finished reading your mail can you please come through to my office, and we can review what needs to be achieved over the next few days?"

◆

Candice looked up from her computer, smiled and said "Good morning Maxine. I'll come through in two minutes, would you like some coffee?"

"Thanks, I'd love some," came the reply. "Please also bring through the report that Richard and James were doing for me. I'd like to read through it before I meet with them later this morning."

As the two women sat down to discuss the priorities for achievement over the next week, Maxine thought, I'm really enjoying seeing how Candice has blossomed over the last few weeks. She is relishing the challenges that I give her, and delivering them with relative ease.

With this realization she said, "You know Candice, you are becoming a very skilled personal assistant without a great deal of input from me."

"I think it's because I'm really enjoying working with you. It's such fun!" the younger woman said, blushing profusely.

As Candice rose to leave the room, Maxine smiled and said, "I agree it's great fun and it's also very rewarding to see you blossoming like this."

Earlier in the day Maxine had called the chairman, and left a message that she needed to speak with him. So while she waited for him to return her call she took the time to review the "report" produced by James and Richard before their scheduled meeting at ten. As she started to read through the rather long document she realized that her initial impressions when she had read it were correct. All of the problems highlighted were deemed to emanate in the operations department and none in

◆

finance. Also all of the identified actions were for the operations department.

There's something amiss here, thought Maxine. Even if everything in the finance department was perfect (and I'm sure it isn't), I would expect both departments to be agreeing joint actions to support each other in remedying the problems. It appears as if Richard has dominated this whole process. I have to get to the bottom of this, and quickly.

As she pondered the situation she was reminded of the importance of creating a win-win. In order for her to achieve that which she desired, (her win) she needed to find a way to create a "win" for Richard and James. Creating the win-win enables everyone to leave a discussion or meeting feeling good. To create the traditional win-lose would mean that someone leaves the meeting feeling bruised and de-motivated. As she contemplated this she asked herself, how do I create a win-win

in this situation? I'm uncertain at this stage, but I must remember to hold this thought during our upcoming meeting.

At the prescribed time, the two men arrived for their meeting. Maxine started by asking them to elaborate on the recommendations they had made. Richard launched into a description of what *he* thought the operations department should be doing. He stated that they had agreed that the finance dead line should stay the same, and that the operations department would now change their schedules to achieve this.

As Maxine listened, she thought, what is going on? Has James allowed Richard to completely steam roller him with this?

As Richard completed his monologue Maxine said "Thanks Richard. James, are you in agreement with all this?"

"Yes," came a very flat reply.

Maxine remained unconvinced so she probed a little deeper. "So, if I understand you correctly, there will be no changes in the finance department, and all the changes will be within the operations department. Is this correct?" she asked. They both nodded.

"OK, so what discussions have you had as to the feasibility of these recommendations with your teams James?" she asked to create an opportunity to check out the reality behind their proposal. "And how is this feeding into the working group on interface between the departments?"

Rather nervously, James cleared his throat and said "Well, actually I haven't discussed it with the teams yet. Richard and I just thought this was the best way forward."

◆

"So, tell me what is your evidence that this will work?" asked Maxine, attempting to hide her frustration.

"Well, they just have to be told," commented Richard.

"Who has to be told what?" asked Maxine calmly.

"Well, the operations people just have to be told what they have to do," he replied with a degree of heightening irritation in his voice.

"Even if it causes them more work?" she asked.

"Well yes, if this is what has been decided!" he replied, his irritation mounting.

"Ok," said Maxine. "I'm stopping this here. What has happened about the working group looking at this? Are you really telling me that your proposals have not been tested with them?"

James nodded rather sheepishly, and Richard looked away.

"So exactly what is happening to the work of the group who are looking at identifying standards to increase the efficiency of processing customer claims?" asked Maxine rather sharply, no

longer attempting to hide her irritation.

"Well, actually we didn't really see the point of the group since James and I had done this report, so I told them not to meet," stated Richard.

"On whose authority?" asked Maxine feeling the rising annoyance in her stomach.

"Well, eermmm mine…" replied Richard, this time a little hesitantly.

"So you're telling me that you chose to overrule a corporate decision made at the Directors Management Team meeting, and implement something new without consultation?" asked an incredulous Maxine. This time both men looked at the floor.

"Let us be clear," said Maxine. "No decisions made at our directors meetings or board meetings can be overruled unilaterally. Otherwise what is the purpose of making those decisions in the first place? Do I make myself crystal clear?"

"Yes," came the mumbled replies.

She continued. "Neither am I happy with directors making decisions without any understanding or testing of the impact of these decisions. James, what do you think will be the impact of the current proposals on your department?"

"Well, errr…..I think that I'll need to change people's shifts," he stammered.

"And what impact will this have on the overall workload of the department?" Maxine asked.

"I'm not really sure, but we will manage somehow," he replied in a tone of voice that lacked any real commitment or enthusiasm.

"Withoutunderstandinghowthiswillimpactontheoverall workload, and without the input of the staff of either department, I'm unwilling to agree to any proposals," said Maxine. She was beginning to get very concerned about the bullying approach of Richard, and James' apparent inability to counter this. No wonder the operations department were completely overloaded and blamed for lack of delivery, their director was allowing it to happen. In the meantime the finance department could sit across the hallway pointing their accusatory fingers.

This situation requires clear direction, and at the same time I need to create a win for James as he clearly feels he has lost to Richard, and yet somehow I also need to keep Richard in the loop. Yes, this presents quite a challenge, she thought.

Collecting her thoughts once more Maxine went on to say, "First of all I want you to go back to the agreement we made at the directors meeting. I then want you to work together to draft a brief for the working group looking at identifying standards to increase the efficiency of processing customer claims as we originally agreed. I wish to see a full brief by the end of today, and at the same time I want you to have identified three volunteers from each of your departments who will be part of this group. The other groups are almost ready to share their findings, and are reporting back by the end of next week. Therefore, you will need to allow people to be released from their normal work in order to do this as a priority. Do you understand?" she asked. They both nodded rather glumly.

"So do either of you have any further questions?"

"Well, what if we can't find volunteers?" asked Richard.

"Let me know, and I'll come and talk to your staff myself," said Maxine. "I'll also attend the first meeting of the group. Candice will clear my diary in order to do this. This is too important to stall at this early stage. So finally, do you have any more questions?"

There was a silence, "Good, I'll expect the outline brief for the group by the end of the day. We will then get this back on track." stated Maxine firmly.

As the two men made their way out of her office Maxine thought about the style and approach she had needed to adopt to achieve an outcome that would be fair and achievable. This meeting had also given her insights into the relationship between

Richard and James. Richard had obviously dominated and even bullied James, who then appeared to simply follow along. She knew that whilst her preferred approach was to facilitate people in identifying the best way forward, sometimes the only way to progress was to be very directive as in this instance. "Different strokes for different folks" Colin's words reverberated around her head.

I need to use all of my own behavioral flexibility here to achieve the results I know we can achieve, she thought quietly.

Then another thought struck her. One of the most important things I learned on that course I recently attended was *the person who demonstrates the most behavioral flexibility is the person who ultimately controls the system.* I'm certainly going to have plenty of opportunities to develop those skills here!

Maxine spent the rest of the day discussing the purpose

and desired outcomes of the board seminar with her chairman. She then sent out the briefing, and had a meeting with key members of staff. She had also tested her ideas about a customer open day and workshop with a few of Extreme Ventures customers. All in all she felt she had a very satisfactory day.

James had asked to see her at the end of the day, and to bring along the proposal for the group looking at increasing the efficiency of processing customer claims. As he sat down James looked really uncomfortable so Maxine asked, "What can I do to help you James?"

He cleared his throat and said very quietly, "I felt that you were very unhappy with the work you had asked Richard and I to do, and that you thought we should, well I..I..." he stuttered, "should be doing things rather differently and..." he paused and took a deep breath.

"Yes," said Maxine, encouragingly, "Your perceptions are spot on correct. I was very concerned that agreements made at directors meetings had simply been ignored. Most importantly, I was concerned that the key people who should have been involved in a fundamental process, had not been given the opportunity. A further concern was that you had not taken into account the impact that the proposed changes would have on the overall workload of your department, nor the individuals involved."

She saw James' face drop, and she smiled saying, "Look, I'm here to help but I'm also here to ensure this organization delivers. So I need you to tell me what you can and cannot do. If

◆

you're open and honest with me we can work together to resolve the issues no matter how difficult they are. Hiding things from me will not work. So given this, what would be helpful for you to talk to me about now?"

"I'm finding it difficult to manage the departmental workload, and everything I do makes things worse! Richard and I have put together the brief for the working group but I'm not sure it really grasps the tasks as we agreed them," he blurted out.

"Well, leave the proposal with me, and I'll look through it and give you comments. In the meantime what other help can I give you?" she asked smiling reassuringly.

Maxine then spent the next thirty minutes talking through the issues of the operations department. Remembering to be directive she suggested that he set aside some time the next day to discuss the departmental performance with his new deputy Susan, and to arrange for the three of them (Maxine, James and Susan) to discuss the issues they had identified later in the week.

"In this way we can agree the priorities and actions required to increase efficiency and staff morale," said Maxine reassuringly.

As James left her office he turned and said, "Thank you Maxine, I really appreciate your help."

Maxine reviewed the proposal James had left with her, and made a few basic modifications, but to her relief it was broadly on track. She was greatly relieved to discover that six volunteers had also been identified for the working group. She then asked Candice to clear the time in her diary in order for her to brief the group personally and answer any questions they had the following day.

Before leaving her office to meet her husband and some friends for dinner, Maxine ran through her action list for the day. Excellent, she thought. There's only one thing on the list I did not achieve and that was my walk about. Hmmm-- I'll make sure I do that on my way into my office tomorrow. There's also one thing I did achieve that was not on the list, and that was being able to start to develop my relationship with James. We took a huge step forward today, and I think we're on the right track. But Richard, now that's a different story!

She then spent a few minutes jotting down her priorities for the next day, closed her notebook put it in her brief case, and closed the door on another interesting day at Extreme Ventures.

Maxine had scheduled the customer service open day two weeks prior to the board strategy workshop as she wanted to ensure that the key issues raised could be incorporated into the development of the strategy and ultimately the business plan.

◆

Candice had organized the day brilliantly. Different groups of people were scheduled to arrive at various times throughout the day. Maxine would start off each session with a short presentation outlining the purpose of the day. She really wanted to understand the needs of their customers, receive their genuine comments, and use the opportunity to explain her thoughts on customer services. It would also provide an ideal opportunity to introduce people to their recently designated customer account manager within the operations department. Maxine and Candice ran through the program together early that morning.

"We have over a hundred people who have said they are coming today," said Candice.

Maxine beamed in acknowledgement of all the preparatory work that had gone into the day and said, "This is wonderful! Now, run me through the logistics."

"Well, I've divided the people into five groups of approximately twenty people" she replied. "Each group has an arrival time between nine thirty in the morning and four in the afternoon. I've also allowed longer between the sessions at lunchtime because we have a further thirty people who have accepted our invitation to lunch. So, I've allowed time for you to talk to people over lunch, and to be able to eat something yourself," she said with a grin.

"Thanks for looking after my stomach," said Maxine, also grinning. "Shall we double check we have everything set up the best that we can?"

The two women double-checked the schedule. Candice had arranged a brief thirty-minute introductory session with Maxine for each group. This enabled her to outline the purpose of the day, and to answer any general questions people had. The team leaders from the operations team would then collect their various visitors and introduce them to their customer account managers. Afterwards if anyone wanted to see someone in the other teams or departments this had been arranged.

"There are a total of fifty-eight people for lunch, so I've organized a finger buffet," said Candice. "People can then chat and eat at the same time. It will also give you a chance to have a more informal discussion with a few of our customers, so you should pick up some more *soft intelligence* as you call it."

"Candice this is brilliant, you really are a star!" said Maxine. "So have you been able to brief everyone else and is everything else ok?"

"Yes, I think everything is ok. Richard was very reluctant to participate though," said Candice. "But James is very enthusiastic, it's the first time I've seen him really smile in a long time."

Another issue with Richard, thought Maxine. He must be feeling very threatened. What do I need to do to enable him to understand that we're shifting to a customer driven organization? It's excellent news about James though, maybe he simply needs to be in a different role. A role in which he can flourish away from direct people management."

The day ran really smoothly, Candice's detailed organization had really paid off. Some customers were noticeably and probably justifiably irritated with the poor standards of service they had been receiving, and one or two had been downright belligerent. But the majority had been very welcoming of Maxine's willingness to listen and take action. Candice had designed some feedback forms, which she was collating to be included in the board development day.

She really does have a flair for this type of activity, thought Maxine. I must think about ways to capitalize on this for her own development, and the good of the company.

The day after the open day Maxine called all the staff together to thank them for their input into the day. It had been a great success; the customers had really appreciated the welcome they received, along with the opportunity to air their concerns. The majority had been relieved and pleased to hear that Extreme Ventures was clearly focusing on improving customer services. There were a few outstanding issues that she would follow up with the various directors.

She concluded by saying, "I want to take this opportunity to thank all of you who participated. We've received some very favorable feedback for having the courage to listen. I was also told that many of you were really helpful and a number of issues have already been resolved. So well done, and thank you, you are at the forefront of Extreme Ventures, and the first line of contact for our customers, as far as they are concerned you are *the company*. I'd also specifically like to thank Candice for all her work in organizing the logistics of the day. She did a great job as all the right people arrived in the right place at the right time, and we didn't lose anyone," said Maxine with a grin. She watched as Candice blushed and glowed as a ripple of

spontaneous applause rang out in the room.

Whoever would have thought this would have happened just a few short weeks ago? she asked herself satisfied that she really was making some genuine progress. My next challenge will be the board development day. It will be interesting to see how that pans out. With Colin facilitating, I'm sure it will be a great success.

A couple of weeks later Maxine was sat at her desk early in the morning reflecting on the events of yet another important day. It had been a significant day in the transformation process for

Extreme Ventures as it had been the first ever board development day in the company's history. Colin had facilitated the day with his usual sense of calm, humor, and highly skilled leadership. This had enabled all of the members, both executives and non-executives, to participate in shaping the overall direction of travel for the company as a whole. He had even managed to engage Richard's participation, despite his rather rude outburst at the beginning of the day.

At Maxine's request Candice had found a pleasant hotel with a relaxed atmosphere for the venue. From past experience Maxine was aware of the importance of being away from the workplace to create a sense of the day being different. This allowed people to dissociate their thinking from their usual day

to day activities and details.

Everyone had arrived by nine thirty, and seemed to be both relaxed, and up beat. This was the first opportunity that the board had taken in the six years since the initial conception of Extreme Ventures to create some fresh and original thinking.

Brian as chairman made a brief, clear and simple introduction. "This is a wonderful opportunity to lift us out from the day to day business of Extreme Ventures, and to undertake some *blue sky* thinking as I believe it's called," he said with a chuckle. "Maxine and I have discussed the importance of creating a way forward that places Extreme Ventures in the forefront of our field, and creates the potential for us to enter into new areas of business from a position of strength, building on a desirable reputation. There's clearly a long way to go but today is the day for us to explore the various possibilities and options. To assist us in this somewhat challenging task we've been fortunate to engage the services of Colin Boothroyd. Colin is a particularly experienced facilitator known for his dynamic and pragmatic style."

Brian then briefly described some of Colin's more notable achievements before handing the floor over to him.

Colin stepped forward, looking as relaxed, and in control as ever. He smiled and explained that the purpose of the day was to establish an agreed strategic direction for Extreme Ventures and to begin to establish the framework for achieving this. Just as he was finishing his introduction Richard interrupted, and said, "I think this is a waste of time and money. I know what I'm doing, and what my staff need to do!"

There were a few audible gasps from around the group, and Maxine thought that it felt as if people were literally holding their breath.

Colin simply stepped forward, smiled, and said "I can understand that you may be feeling frustrated at the moment. However, in my experience I know how important it is to have the finance director at a day such as this. Your input will be invaluable in assessing the financial risk of any proposals that are generated throughout the day."

"Yes, but…" Richard interjected.

"Please just allow me to finish," said Colin gently and firmly. "Having had the pleasure of working with many boards of directors I know how important it is to set aside time like this to establish a clear direction for the organization as a whole. As you're aware, board directors have a corporate responsibility, which is wider than their own departments. I therefore know that your input is both important and necessary."

A great example of creating a win-win, thought Maxine. Richard sat back in his chair, and she saw out of the corner of her

eye Brian visibly relaxing.

"I suggest," continued Colin "that you may wish to see the day through and then at the end we can review any concerns you still have. Is this ok with you?"

"Yes, that's fine," said Richard. He looked somewhat confused at being led so gracefully out of his original attack.

Colin had continued by inviting people to identify personal outcomes for the day. Maxine smiled inwardly as she looked towards Richard and thought, well done, Colin. As ever, you handled a potentially difficult situation with grace and ease. You didn't even flinch, and Richard is now being as good as gold.

Maxine, Brian, and Colin had agreed a simple agenda for the day focusing on two key steps:

1.*Setting the context* – identifying the current situation, organizational strengths and areas for improvement (with input

from the diagonal slice groups).

2. *Looking ahead* – the strategic vision for Extreme Ventures in five years time.

Maxine was pleased with the amount of energy and enthusiasm the board members put into the day, and was delighted with the clear way forward that had been achieved by the end. Even Richard had a hint of a sparkle in his eyes. He genuinely seemed to relish the opportunities given by Colin to assess the organizational risks despite the fact that not one of the objections he had identified were insurmountable nor could not be overcome.

She now felt that she had a clear brief to take the organization forward. The goal was to place Extreme Ventures within the top quartile of performance within their business sector, rather than its current position very close to the bottom.

Once this had been achieved the next step was to offer additional complementary services to customers based on their feedback. The feedback from the diagonal slice working groups had been invaluable to the discussions. The members were so impressed with the work of these groups that Maxine had suggested that, the Chairman send an e-mail to all participants personally thanking them for their contributions. Brain had gladly agreed to do this.

As she sat reflecting, Maxine was putting together her briefing for the staff, outlining the direction of travel and agreements reached yesterday. She would use this as an opportunity to describe how personal work objectives and personal development plans would fit within this new framework. She was also establishing a program of regular updates as the work progressed. These updates would provide the opportunity for her to listen to any concerns or views from the staff, and to take steps to ameliorate these wherever possible.

LEARNING POINTS

➤ At the beginning of each
day set your priorities for
the day in order of importance and at the end
of the day review your progress. Have no more
than six priorities each day.

➤ Seek to create a win-win in every
situation. This enables everyone to leave a
meeting feeling good.

➤ Clarify, clarify, and clarify, all lines of
accountability for all actions and decisions.

➤ Always check that your message has been
understood by asking genuine open questions to
clarify.

➤ The person who demonstrates the most
behavioral flexibility is the person who
ultimately controls the situation.

➤ Be available and accessible to
staff, giving them to access the
support that they need.

➤ Listen to your customers; they know what they want.

➤ A genuine 'thank you' reinforces the value of your staff and enhances their motivation.

➤ Select a venue away from your work site for facilitated workshops. This creates an atmosphere, which supports the free thinking required to be creative.

➤ Never respond to an attack with a defense or counter attack. Offer a measured and firm response, which offers a graceful step down for the attacker.

➤ Keep agendas clear and simple (remember KISS, Keep It Simple Stupid).

➤ Keep staff informed of developments as they arise throughout any change process and be open to receive any feedback.

6

Barefoot in the Boardroom

Maxine looked around the room, "It's hard to believe I've really been here two years," she said to Candice. "The time really seems to have flown."

"So much has happened in that time," replied Candice. "If you had told me at the beginning all that you would have achieved by now, I'd never have believed you. I've never had such fun at work before either," she said, beaming.

"I could not have done a lot of this without your support you know," said Maxine also smiling as she saw the younger woman's pride and satisfaction.

She looked around her office, which she had made bright, light and comfortable, somewhat different from the oppressiveness of the office she had inherited. As she glanced around the room her eyes settled on the beautiful bouquet of flowers that had been waiting for her on her arrival that morning. They were a wonderful second anniversary surprise from her team.

In the last two years Extreme Ventures had been completely reorganized to support the needs of their customers, placing customer service at the heart of their business. Maxine reflected on how the various directors had responded to these challenges. Jill had struggled in the early part of Maxine's tenure

◆

but had soon begun to blossom under her leadership. So much so, that Maxine found she needed to provide less and less guidance, and was able to delegate much more to her. The result of this was that Jill was leading her contracts team more effectively, and able to delegate considerably more to her increasingly competent team.

The operations department had undergone major restructuring with multifunctional teams providing complete packages of support to their customers. Initially there was a good deal of skepticism but this had been overcome by listening to people's concerns. The concept of customer account managers had been heartily welcomed by the customers and staff alike. All the piles of paper had disappeared and walking into the operations department was now a pleasure. Susan had responded very well to her new role as director when James moved to take the role of Associate Chief Executive for Customer Services. This would probably be a short-term position for him whilst the concept of customer services was woven into the fabric of the organization in every job and activity. However, in the meantime James played a very important role in signaling to the customers and staff alike the importance of all customers to Extreme Ventures. His easy and approachable style was ideal for handling customer queries and concerns. He had made great strides in standing firm on the issues he believed in. This had enabled him to be significantly instrumental in facilitating substantial parts of the change management process, providing valuable customer input.

Richard had recently left the organization to undertake a

role within a local charity where he could do his work without the need to interact with customers or many staff. Graham Wilson who had been appointed to replace him came from a strong customer service background. This he combined with a dry sense of humor and sharp wit, and was already proving his value to the organization. Just before Richard had resigned Maxine had received a deputation from his staff to say that they had misunderstood the purpose of the reorganization of the business, and that they could see how much happier people were in the other departments. They also said that they had identified a number of places where processes and procedures could be improved in both the finance and information teams. Maxine suspected that this rebellion by his staff was a contributing factor in Richard's decision to leave. Further contributing factors were Richard's resistance to becoming a corporate player, and his continued evasion of their customers. He had wanted to deal with every query by post so Maxine had asked him to look at the cost differential between telephone answered queries and written responses using conventional mail. He had found that the evidence confirmed that most queries were resolved more quickly and effectively by phone. This saved both time and money, something he had not been happy to admit.

The finance and information teams had begun to identify areas to increase their efficiency, and to pilot these before Graham arrived. This enabled him to work with them to fine-tune the processes and procedures in line with Extreme Ventures goal of placing the customer at the heart of the organization.

Candice had been an invaluable support to Maxine

◆

throughout the two-year period. She had also demonstrated a keen interest in customer services and so provided some direct part-time support to James. Her pleasant manner and efficiency were ideal for the role, and gave her the needed opportunity to grow and develop.

Last week Maxine had another coaching session with Colin. She has used this opportunity to prepare for her annual performance appraisal. During their session, Colin had asked her to list her achievements since she joined Extreme Ventures as Chief Executive two years ago.

"Wow," she said. "That's a tough one."

"So lets just map it out on a flip chart," he replied.

She took a deep breath and started to list her achievements:

- The development of the corporate strategy to place customers at the heart of our business.
- Lifting Extreme Ventures from the bottom of the performance league into the top three in the country.
- Engaging all of the staff in the successful implementation of the change management process.
- Establishing clear lines of accountability and reporting.
- Establishing an annual business plan with key milestones for reporting.
- Implementing a process for performance monitoring and personal development planning.
- Establishing an open system of staff briefings and developing my soft intelligence antennae to test the organizational thermometer.

She said this last one with an impish smile on her face.

"What is the smile about?" asked Colin

"Just saying those things makes me feel good inside," she said. "The staff have responded to the challenges so brilliantly, and do you know what the key has really been?"

"Do tell me," he replied, grinning at her obvious delight and success.

"It has simply been by treating people *as people*. Getting to know them, their names, and a little bit about their lives out of work, has paid such huge dividends in turning the organization around.

"I thought that would be the hardest part but actually I enjoyed it and so did the staff. It really seems to have made all the difference in the world. We are after all people, and if we're valued and understood it makes all our lives that little bit easier. I used to think all this stuff was a bit soppy, but I've come to realize that this is far more important than all the other things people get hung up about.

"You know Colin, it has been really hard work at times over the past two years, and yet it has been the most rewarding in my career. I've learned so much, I know there's still a great deal more to learn but I know I've climbed a mountain and so have my teams. I feel like I've really grown up during these two years from a new chief executive starting out on an exciting journey to someone who has made at least part of the journey, and thoroughly enjoyed the experience."

"You have done some tremendous work Maxine, it's a real tribute to your tenacity and vision that Extreme Ventures has come so far. What I'd like to know is what do you think has been your greatest achievement?" Colin asked prodding her to become more specific.

"Well, I have to say it has been the turn around in our market position from close to the very bottom to number three in the country. All the other achievements have supported this one," she replied.

"And what have you learned from all of this?" he asked with another grin

"I've learned that:

- An organization is nothing without its people, and getting the right people in the right position is fundamental to it's success.
- The more I listen to people and weigh all of the views and perspectives, then apply my own discernment, the better my decisions.
- The more flexible my behavior the easier it has been to get things done, a good example of this has been growing my team and managing them in the best way for them. Moving them through the directing, guiding and delegating cycle.
- Looking after myself mentally, emotionally, physically, and spiritually enables me to ride the storms with more ease than I would have imagined.
- Doing what I love and loving what I do is wonderful!

"So what next?" asked Colin.

"Ah," she replied, "Now that's another story!"

◆

Lightning Source UK Ltd.
Milton Keynes UK
30 September 2010

160595UK00003B/298/P